This igloo book belongs to:

igloobooks

Published in 2020
First published in the UK by Igloo Books Ltd
An imprint of Igloo Books Ltd
Cottage Farm, NN6 0BJ, UK
Owned by Bonnier Books
Sveavägen 56, Stockholm, Sweden
www.igloobooks.com

1120 006
6 8 10 11 9 7 5
ISBN 978-1-78557-736-9

Written by Melanie Joyce
Illustrated by Jenny Wren

Cover designed by Richard Sykes
Interiors designed by Kerri-Ann Hulme
Edited by Nataila Boileau

Printed and manufactured in China

Princess Snow and the Unicorn

igloobooks

Long ago, in a kingdom of winter, there lived a princess called Snow. She loved her cold and frosty home, but Snow didn't have any friends and was very lonely.

One day, her mother, the Ice Queen, gave the sad princess a beautiful snow globe. "Sometimes, all you need is a little magic," said the queen, with a smile.

Snow looked into the globe. She saw ice maidens and fairies. She saw snowmen and a princess with a golden tiara, riding a beautiful unicorn.

"I wish that was me," said Snow, shaking the globe so the snowflakes swirled and danced. Suddenly, the princess felt like she was swirling and spinning, down, down, until...

... Snow found herself in a magical world. Fairies fluttered around her and a shining unicorn shook his mane as tiny fairy bells tinkled. "I'm inside the globe," gasped Snow.

"Yes, Princess," said the unicorn, "because you wished it so."
The fairies fluttered around excitedly. "We'll be your friends!"
they cried, giggling.

The fairies lifted the princess onto the back of the unicorn. Up, up they flew, over fields and hedges thick with snow, over a sparkling palace to a frozen lake where snowmen stood.

"How sweet they are," said the princess. She touched
their frosty noses and the fairy bells jingled. One snowman
blinked and then another. "Hello, Princess," they said.
"Come and dance with us."

Magical instruments played sweet music and the snowmen began to sway. They held Snow's hand and danced in a circle. With each step, they moved faster and faster.

Round and round they flew, jigging and whirling to the enchanting music.

The unicorn shook his mane and the fairy bells jingled.
The snowmen stood still, as four beautiful ice maidens glided
across the lake. They bowed and gently took Snow's hand.

The princess twirled and danced as if she were a graceful ballerina, elegantly holding her arms like the wings of a beautiful swan.

Once more, the unicorn shook his mane and Snow found herself on his back. "To the rainbow!" cried the fairies, as they swooshed upwards. "Goodbye!" called Snow.

Far above the clouds arched a beautiful rainbow.
The fairies collected icicles from the clouds and dipped them
into the rainbow to make gems to decorate Snow's hair.

"How beautiful," said Snow, as the gems glittered in the sunlight. "I wish I could show my mother." The unicorn shook his mane and the magic bells tinkled. "As you wish, Princess," he said.

Suddenly, it began to snow. Thick flakes fell as the unicorn flew down, down. "Goodbye, Princess," said the faint voices of the fairies as they disappeared into the swirling curtain.

"Goodbye," said the unicorn, softly.
"Remember, we will always be your friends."
"Thank you," said Snow, as she watched the whirling
flakes spinning all around.

The princess felt like she was spinning as well.
Down, down and far below, someone was
calling her name. "Snow, Snow..."

"Snow, wake up," said the Ice Queen. Princess Snow gave
her mother the biggest hug, cuddling into her soft cape.
"The snow globe is amazing," she said.

"Yes, it's magic," said the queen, smiling as she helped the princess into her beautiful sleigh. Snow looked into the enchanted snow globe. "Now I will always have friends," she said, as the sleigh sped off across the glittering ice.